HOOK

ED YOUNG

A NEAL PORTER BOOK
ROARING BROOK PRESS
NEW YORK

To Eugene Winick,
my wise advisor and dedicated fellow TC student
and loyal friend

A Neal Porter Book
Published by Roaring Brook Press
Roaring Brook Press is a division of Holtzbrinck Publishing Holdings Limited Partnership
175 Fifth Avenue, New York, New York 10010

www.roaringbrookpress.com

Distributed in Canada by H. B. Fenn and Company, Ltd.

Cataloging-in-Publication Data is on file at the Library of Congress.
ISBN: 978-1-59643-363-2

Roaring Brook Press books are available for special promotions and premiums.
For details contact: Director of Special Markets, Holtzbrinck Publishers.

Printed in December 2009 in China by South China Printing Co. Ltd., Dongguan City, Guangdong Province
Book design by Jennifer Browne
First edition May 2009
4 6 8 10 9 7 5 3

An abandoned egg.

A young boy.

When?

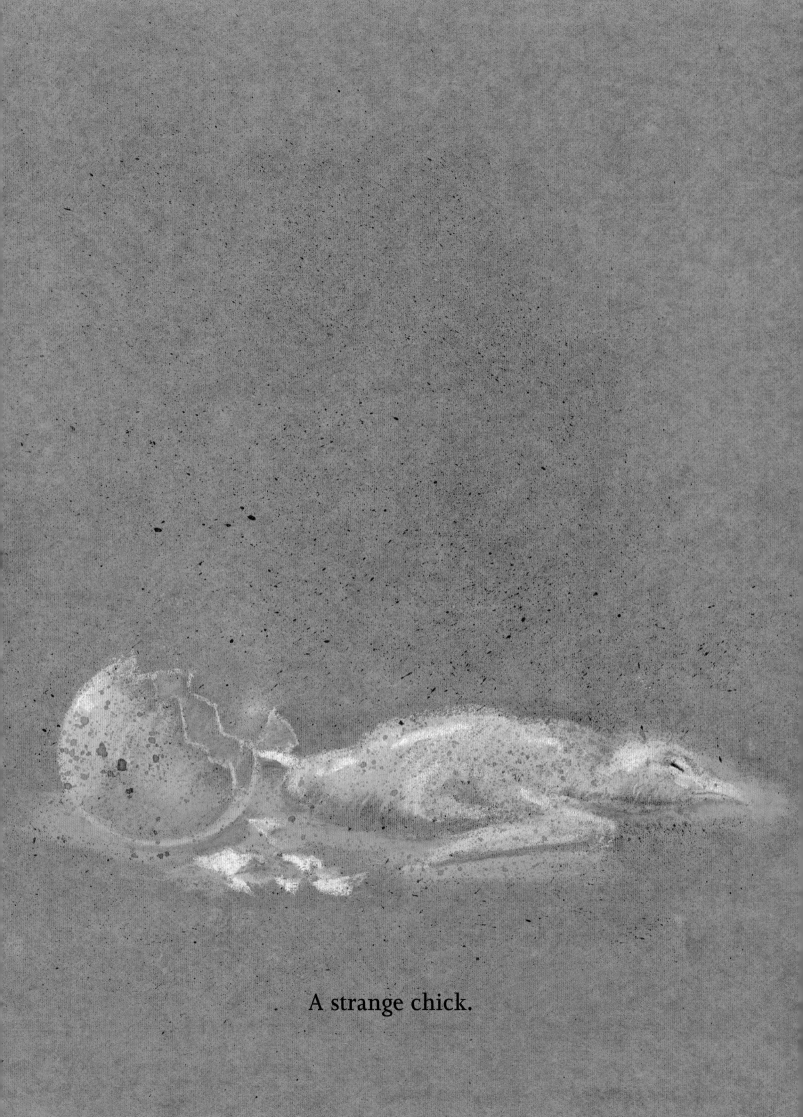

A strange chick.

A hook nose?

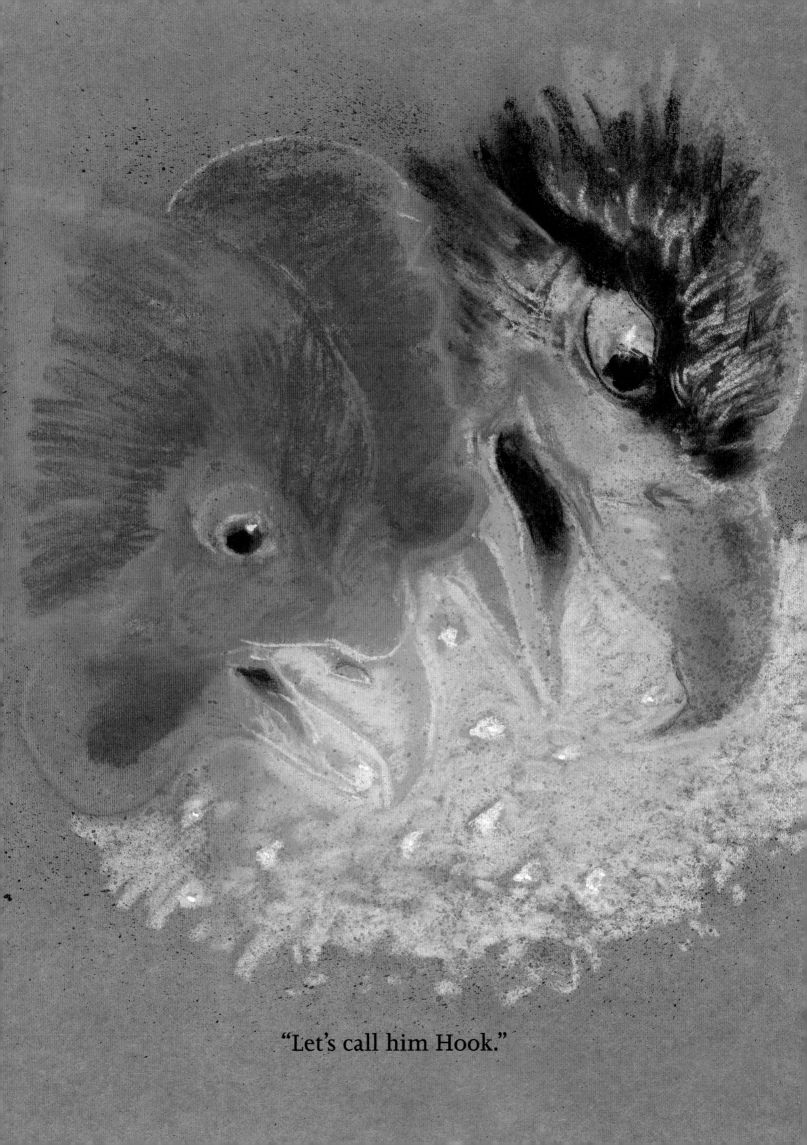

"Let's call him Hook."

Kicking up a storm.

Looking back.

"You are not meant for earth."

A higher place.

He pushes off, but falls to earth.

A short first flight.

She asks for help.

An even higher place.

Another try.

Another fall.

"We'll try again, Hook."

They start off before daybreak.

This time in the great canyon.

Hook plunges.

He spreads his wings,
catching a gust of air.

And rises to where he belongs . . .

For he wasn't meant for earth.